Robert Munsch

MUD PUDDLE

Illustrated by
Dušan Petričić

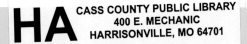

HA CASS COUNTY PUBLIC LIBRARY
400 E. MECHANIC
HARRISONVILLE, MO 64701

0 0022 0440760 1

annick press
toronto + new york + vancouver

© 1979, 2012 Bob Munsch Enterprises Ltd. (text)
© 2012 Dušan Petričić (illustrations)
Designed by Sheryl Shapiro
Third printing, November 2013

Annick Press Ltd.
All rights reserved. No part of this work covered by the copyrights hereon may be reproduced or used in any form or by any means—graphic, electronic, or mechanical—without the prior written permission of the publisher.

We acknowledge the support of the Canada Council for the Arts, the Ontario Arts Council, and the Government of Canada through the Canada Book Fund (CBF) for our publishing activities.

 ONTARIO ARTS COUNCIL
CONSEIL DES ARTS DE L'ONTARIO

Cataloging in Publication

Munsch, Robert N., 1945-
    Mud puddle / Robert Munsch ; illustrated by Dušan Petričić. — Anniversary ed., Classic Munsch.

ISBN 978-1-55451-426-7 (pbk.). — ISBN 978-1-55451-427-4 (bound)

    I. Petričić, Dušan II. Title.

PS8576.U575M84 2012   jC813'.54   C2012-900571-1

Distributed in Canada by:
Firefly Books Ltd.
50 Staples Avenue, Unit 1
Richmond Hill, ON
L4B 0A7

Published in the U.S.A. by Annick Press (U.S.) Ltd.
Distributed in the U.S.A. by:
Firefly Books (U.S.) Inc.
P.O. Box 1338
Ellicott Station
Buffalo, NY 14205

Printed in China

Visit us at: www.annickpress.com
Visit Robert Munsch at: www.robertmunsch.com

To Jeffrey
—R.M.
In memory of my mother
—D.P.

Jule Ann's mother bought her clean new clothes. Jule Ann put on a clean new shirt and buttoned it up the front. She put on clean new pants and buttoned them up the front.

Then she walked outside and sat down under the apple tree.

Unfortunately, hiding up in the
apple tree there was a mud puddle.
It saw Jule Ann sitting there and it
jumped right on her head.

She got completely all over muddy.
Even her ears were full of mud.

Jule Ann ran inside, yelling,
**"Mommy, Mommy! A mud puddle
jumped on me."**

Her mother picked her up, took off all her
clothes, and dropped her into a tub of water.

She scrubbed Jule Ann till she was red all over.

She washed out her ears.
She washed out her eyes.
She even washed out her mouth.

Jule Ann put on a clean new shirt and buttoned it up the front. She put on clean new pants and buttoned them up the front.

Then she looked out the back door. She couldn't see a mud puddle anywhere, so she walked outside and sat down in her sandbox.

The sandbox was next to the house, and hiding up on top of the house there was a mud puddle.

It saw Jule Ann sitting down there and it jumped right on her head. She got completely all over muddy. Even her nose was full of mud.

Jule Ann ran inside, yelling, **"Mommy, Mommy! A mud puddle jumped on me."**

Jule Ann's mother picked her up, took off all her clothes, and dropped her into a tub of water.

She scrubbed Jule Ann till she was red all over.

She washed out her ears.
She washed out her eyes.
She washed out her mouth.
She even washed out her nose.

Jule Ann put on a clean new shirt
and buttoned it up the front.
Then she put on clean new pants
and buttoned them up the front.

Then she had an idea. She reached
way back into the closet and got
a big yellow raincoat. She put it
on and walked outside.

There was no mud puddle anywhere, so she yelled, **"Hey, Mud Puddle!"**

Nothing happened, so she yelled even louder, **"Hey, Mud Puddle!!"**

Jule Ann was standing in the sunshine in her raincoat, getting very hot. She pulled back her hood. Nothing happened. She took off her raincoat.

As soon as she took off her coat, out from behind the doghouse there came the mud puddle. It ran across the grass and jumped right on Jule Ann's head. She got completely all over muddy.

Jule Ann ran inside, yelling,
**"Mommy, Mommy! A mud puddle
jumped on me."**

Her mother picked her up, took off all her
clothes, and dropped her into a tub full of water.

She scrubbed Jule Ann till she was red all over.

She washed out her ears.
She washed out her eyes.
She washed out her mouth.
She washed out her nose.
She even washed out her belly button.

Jule Ann put on a clean new shirt and buttoned it up the front. She put on clean new pants and buttoned them up the front.

Then she sat by the back door because she was afraid to go outside.

Then she had an idea.

She reached up to the sink and took a bar of smelly yellow soap. She gave it a smell—yecch! She took another bar of smelly yellow soap and gave it a smell—yecch! She put the smelly yellow soap in her pockets.

Then she ran out into the middle
of the backyard and yelled,

"Hey, Mud Puddle!"

The mud puddle jumped over the
fence and ran right toward her.

Jule Ann threw a bar of soap right into the
mud puddle's middle. The mud puddle stopped.

Jule Ann threw the other bar of soap right into the mud puddle. The mud puddle said, "Awk, yecch, wackh!"

It ran across the grass, jumped over
the fence, and never came back.

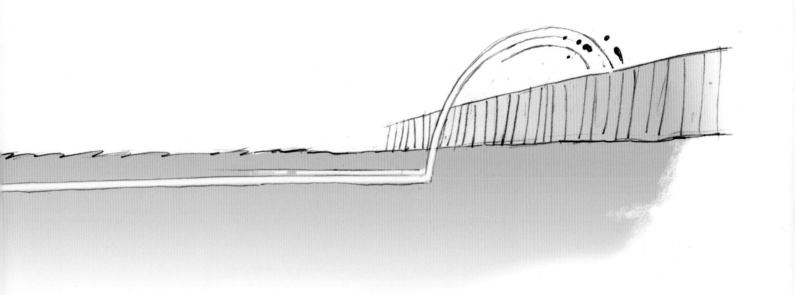

Other books in the Munsch for Kids series:

The Dark
The Paper Bag Princess
The Boy in the Drawer
Jonathan Cleaned Up—Then He Heard a Sound
Murmel, Murmel, Murmel
Millicent and the Wind
Mortimer
The Fire Station
Angela's Airplane
David's Father
Thomas' Snowsuit
50 Below Zero
I Have to Go!
Moira's Birthday
A Promise Is a Promise
Pigs
Something Good
Show and Tell
Purple, Green and Yellow
Wait and See
Where Is Gah-Ning?
From Far Away
Stephanie's Ponytail
Munschworks: The First Munsch Collection
Munschworks 2: The Second Munsch Treasury
Munschworks 3: The Third Munsch Treasury
Munschworks 4: The Fourth Munsch Treasury
The Munschworks Grand Treasury
Munsch Mini-Treasury One
Munsch Mini-Treasury Two

Many Munsch titles are available in French and/or
Spanish. Please contact your favorite supplier.